Granny! Granny!

Where are you?

For Zaki

First American edition published in 2010
by Boxer Books Limited.

Distributed in the United States and Canada by
Sterling Publishing Co., Inc.
387 Park Avenue South, New York, NY 10016-8810

First published in Great Britain in 2010
by Boxer Books Limited.
www.boxerbooks.com

The illustrations were prepared using an ink line and watercolor on handmade paper.
The text is set in Adobe Garamond.

ISBN 978-1-906250-91-1

1 3 5 7 9 10 8 6 4 2

Printed in China

All of our papers are sourced from managed forests and renewable resources.

What's the Matter, Bunny Blue?

Nicola Smee

Boxer Books

What's the matter, Bunny Blue?

I've lost my Granny!
BOO HOO HOO!

What does she look like, Bunny Blue?

She's got twinkly eyes!
BOO HOO HOO!

What else does she look like, Bunny Blue?

She's got a BIG smile!
BOO HOO HOO!

Can you give us another clue?

She's got soft, furry arms!
BOO HOO HOO!

Is she, by any chance, blue like you?

Oh yes, she is!
BOO HOO HOO!

Does she happen to be missing a shoe?

I don't know!
BOO HOO HOO!

She can't have
gone far, Bunny Blue.
We'll all come along
and search with you.

THERE you are, my Bunny Blue!

Granny! Granny!
I've FOUND you . . .

. . . and I'm going to
stick to you
like GLUE!

Now let's go home, my Bunny Blue.

Granny, Granny,
I love you.

I love you too,
my Bunny Blue.